BOYS ARE WONDERFUL

A Motivational Book for Boys about Courage, Strength and Self-Awareness | Collection of Short Stories | Present for Boys

Amber A. Adams

ISBN - 9798358104044

THIS BOOK BELONGS TO

....

....

CONTENTS

THE GREEDY KING

Micah was a young boy who lived in the kingdom of Amon. He had lived there his whole life and he loved the castle and the town in the valley below. He loved the people of Amon more than anything and he wanted nothing more than to serve them.

When he was only ten years old, he was given the best opportunity of his life. Each year, the king of Amon chose five boys from the town to serve the kingdom. This year, Micah was chosen as one of the five.

He was given a robe of dark blue and a cap that matched it. Then, a bag with a golden string that he wore over his shoulder. Then, a beautiful horse with a saddle of blue velvet that matched his robe and cap. His job, on the first day of each week, was to go to all the villages of the land and collect donations in his bag.

The people of Amon, you see, were the kindest people on the whole Earth. Most kingdoms needed taxes to fix the roads and feed the poor, but not Amon. The people of Amon gave money freely when they saw a problem that needed fixing in their land.

If a highway broke apart and carriages were running off the road, the people of Amon would come together and fix it. If a child was sick and needed expensive medicine, the people of Amon would come together and raise the money to buy the medicine. Everything that was wrong in the kingdom of Amon could be made right by the goodwill and thankful hearts of the people.

That is why Micah loved to work for the kingdom. He would ride from village to village on his beautiful horse with his beautiful bag and call to the people in their houses. "Money for the poor!" or "Let's fix the road!" or "We have to build a new gate!"

The people would run out of their homes and throw gold coins in his bag. When the bag became full and too heavy to carry, he would return to the castle and empty the coins into the treasury. Usually, he was able to fill three or four bags in one day.

Micah loved his job.

Today, he arrived at the treasury and found the king inside. The treasury was a humongous room with thick iron doors. Only two keys could open these doors, and when Micah got his job serving the kingdom, he was given one of these keys. The king had the other.

The king was standing in the middle of the room when Micah came in and he had the biggest smile on his face. "Look at all of this!" he called to Micah. Micah emptied his bag of coins into a nearby chest and walked over to join the king.

The king was right to be amazed—the treasury was a truly magnificent place. The walls were lined with chests of gold and the most beautiful jewels you have ever seen. There were glimmering swords with golden hilts and necklaces with the most precious gems on Earth. Micah felt lucky to have the key to such a beautiful room.

"Isn't it wonderful!" the king said. "All of this is mine!" He picked up a gold coin and tossed it into the air, letting it fall to the ground with a satisfying tinkle.

Micah nodded and smiled at the king. It was quite wonderful. "So much money," he said, "to help so many people."

The king stopped smiling for one second and then smiled again. He picked up another gold coin and handed it to Micah. "This is for you," he said, "because you do your job so well."

Micah didn't take the coin. He didn't need money. This job was something he did out of the kindness of his heart. It was the best job in all the land and he didn't need to get paid. "I don't need money," he told the king. "The money is for the poor and the roads. The money is meant to help the people of Amon who need it. *I* don't need it."

The king laughed. "Everyone needs money, boy. Look at me! I have all of this and still I need more. Take this coin."

Micah knew it was not his place to ignore the wishes of the king of all the land, so he took the coin and put it in his pocket.

That month, a famine came upon the land of Amon. The rain never came and the crops began to wither and die. Some of the people began to worry, but those who had lived in Amon for a long time knew that everything would be just fine.

In another land, this would have been a big problem, but not in Amon. The people gave more of their money than ever before and the king sent out merchants and traders to buy food from places far away. This food lasted until the famine passed and the crops grew once more.

The next month, a new problem came. As if all the rain had been stored up in the clouds during the famine, it rained harder than ever before on the land of Amon. Some rain is good, but too much rain can be a disaster.

The rain came down like it never had before for thirty long days. When it finally stopped and the people were able to come out of their homes, they saw that the crops were destroyed once again and the whole land was washed away.

This would have been a great problem in another land, but not in Amon. The people gave all they could and the king sent merchants and traders to buy food from other lands.

During this time of rain and famine, Micah worked more than he had ever worked. Almost every day of the week, he rode out on his horse to gather money to help the kingdom. He rode through the intense heat of the famine and the terrible mud of the rain storms. It was all necessary for the people of Amon, so he did it without complaining.

After the rain was over, the people of Amon thought that all would be well again. They went back to their work with smiles on their faces, ready to grow new crops and build the kingdom back to its former glory.

Micah rode out every week just as he had before, and the people gave with smiles on their faces. They didn't have as much to give, but they gave all they could because they knew that they had to rebuild their broken land.

One day, Micah returned from a trip with a bag full of coins and found the king in the treasury once again. He was standing in the same place as before, but this time, his face was different. He no longer had a big smile on his face. His hands were covering his eyes, and it almost seemed as if he was crying.

Micah saw why. The treasury was not like it was before. The walls were no longer stacked with chests of gold, and there were not so many beautiful jewels. Compared to a couple of months earlier, the room looked empty.

It wasn't even close to empty, of course, but it looked that way.

Micah walked up behind the king and cleared his throat so he did not scare him with his presence. "Is everything all right, your majesty?" he asked.

The king turned to him with a frown. "Does it look like everything is all right? Look at this room. Where has everything gone? I'm no longer a rich king! I'm just a normal king!"

Micah smiled. "Of course you are a rich king, your majesty. The land of Amon has been through a terrible couple of months. Without the money from the treasury, where would we be? We would have all starved."

The king nodded slowly. "The land of Amon has been through some hard times and I have had enough. The treasury has saved us twice, but if a third disaster strikes, I'm afraid we don't have enough."

Micah looked around at the remaining money. It was definitely enough for one more famine—maybe even two. "If disaster strikes again, your majesty, you know as well as anyone that the people of Amon will be there to give as much as they can."

The king scowled. "I don't care how much they give. If the land of Amon has any more problems, the treasury will not provide."

"But sir," said Micah, "the treasury is the people's money!"

"When the people give money, whom do they give it to? Me, Micah. It is my decision what is done with the money. It's my money. You are just a boy and I am a king. If there is another issue in the land of Amon, the people can figure it out themselves."

Micah was worried for the land of Amon. He saw that the foolish king meant every word he said.

The next month, disaster did strike. A horrible tornado tore through all the land and the crops were destroyed once again.

The people gave all the money they had because they trusted that the king would use their money to help the whole land.

But weeks passed, and nothing happened. No merchants or traders were sent out. No food came from lands far away.

After a while, the people began to ask where their money had gone. Surely the king had some great plan that would feed them all. But no. The money piled up in the treasury and the greedy king did nothing.

One day, Micah returned from collecting donations and found the king in the treasury once again. These days, it was very difficult for him to fill even one bag with gold coins. The people just didn't have money to give.

The king was staring at the gold in the treasury and he was smiling once again. The treasury was full and the walls were covered in chests of gold just like before. "Isn't it wonderful!" he cried aloud. "I've never seen anything like it."

"But the people are starving, sir!" yelled Micah. "Don't you care?"

"I helped them twice!" said the king. "It's time for them to help themselves."

"But it's their money!" Micah was very upset. "They trust you to use their money to help everyone."

The king grabbed Micah and pushed him towards the door. "I'm king here, boy. You're just a child. Get out of my treasury and give me your key."

Micah knew that he was supposed to listen to the king of all the land, but his heart told him not to. He turned and ran away as fast as he could, holding onto the key with all of his might. The king yelled at the guards to stop him, but Micah was too quick. He was out the door and onto the busy street before anyone could stand in his way.

The people of Amon were no longer happy and Micah knew he had to do something about it before the whole land starved. He had the key to the treasury and that is all he needed. He also knew that the king would be guarding the treasury with many guards.

One night, when the moon was covered by a cloud and all the kingdom was asleep, Micah snuck into the kingdom and slipped into the treasury before anyone could notice. He took his bag and filled it with gold coins, then snuck out.

In the morning, he got on his horse and rode out into all the land, giving back the gold to those who had given it. Then, he returned to the treasury when it was dark, took more gold, and rode out once more.

He did this many, many times until all the gold that had been given to the king was returned to the people. The people went out into the surrounding lands and bought grain and meat to feed their families.

The king tried to catch the unknown thief, but Micah was too quick and cunning. He came in the night like a shadow and left without a sound.

Micah knew that he was not supposed to go against the king of all the land, but he also knew that the people were starving and the king was greedy. He knew that in order to put an end to the evils of the world, you must ignore the rules sometimes.

HOW TO BE BRAVE

If you could be one animal, what would you choose? Maybe a bird so you can fly. Maybe a bug so you can fit in small places. Maybe a mouse or a gopher so you can go underground. Or, maybe a lion.

Lions have it really easy. They aren't afraid of anything. They always have friends and work together. And, they even know how to have fun. Being a lion must be the best of all. With nothing to worry about, you can do whatever you want. Lions are the bravest of all animals.

For Lewis, being a lion wasn't so easy. He loved to roar and he loved to run. He loved to chase his friends and play pranks on other animals. But he had just one problem: he wasn't brave. To be a lion, you must be brave. It doesn't matter if you are a small lion or a big lion. It doesn't matter if you are a boy lion or a girl lion. It doesn't matter how loud you can roar or how fast you can run. All that matters is that you are brave.

Lewis knew this, but he still wasn't brave. He was almost two years old now and he was still scared of the dark and the hyenas that he heard at night. When thunder clouds rolled across the plains of Africa and lightning shot down from the sky, Lewis the lion was scared.

For a human or another animal, this would not be a problem. But for Lewis, this meant that he wasn't a good lion.

Knowing that he would never be accepted as a true lion, Lewis set out to discover how to be brave. If he wasn't naturally brave like all the other lions were, he would teach himself to be brave.

The next day, when the leader of the pride asked for volunteers for the hunt, Lewis the lion raised his shaking paw high into the air. His parents and all of his friends looked very surprised, but Lewis tried to act as if it was completely normal. He smiled as if to say, *why are you looking at me, guys? I love to hunt.*

That night, the hunt went very well. Lewis was told to run around the left side of the herd of gazelles in order to scare them back towards the rest of the lions. He did his job perfectly and they got enough food for many days. When he returned to the pride, his parents and friends were very proud of him. This made him happy.

In the morning, when he awoke, he felt better than ever. *I like being brave,* he thought to himself. He still didn't feel brave, but he knew that if he acted brave, he would begin to feel brave.

That day, the leader of the pride asked for volunteers again. This time, there was a herd of hyenas prowling around the edge of their territory and they needed to scare them away.

Lewis the lion hated hyenas more than anything. They made this high-pitched yapping sound that drove him crazy and their teeth were as sharp as knives. But he knew that a brave lion would not be afraid of the hyenas, so he raised his shaking paw into the air again.

His parents and friends looked very surprised and Lewis smiled again.

This expedition went just as smoothly as the one before, and soon, all the hyenas were yipping and yapping and running away as fast as they could. Lewis had acted very bravely and the leader of the pride smiled at him and patted him on the back. "You did well, Lewis." This made Lewis proud. The leader of the pride rarely gave compliments, so when he did, they meant a lot.

Lewis was happy with himself the next day. He still didn't feel brave, but the hunt and the hyena chase had given him more confidence. He thought that if he volunteered for one more brave expedition, he would surely feel brave.

A week passed and all was peaceful in the lion territory. No hyenas were heard at night and the pride had plenty of food to eat. Lewis enjoyed the peace more than anything, but he knew that he was still not a brave lion and this made him upset. He wanted one more adventure so he could prove to himself and to everyone that he was a brave lion.

The next day, his wish came true. A group of cheetah brothers had roamed into the lions' territory and it was time to show them who was boss. When the leader of the pride asked for volunteers, Lewis raised his paw into the air. His paw still shook and his parents and friends still looked at him a bit surprised, but he smiled. He knew that after today he would be a brave lion. After today he wouldn't be afraid of anything.

That night, when they ambushed the cheetahs, things went well, but not perfect. The lions caught the cheetahs napping, but when they attacked, the leader of the pride got hurt. After the cheetahs were gone, the lions gathered around their leader. He was lying on the ground with a nasty cut on his side.

He told the lions to carry him back to camp, and they did so, setting him by the fire. The whole pride gathered around him, congratulating him for his wonderful victory and wishing him a speedy recovery. They were all just happy he was going to be okay and that the cheetahs were now gone.

Lewis was happy as well, but something was bothering him. He had acted very bravely during the attack on the cheetah camp. He had chased and roared and scratched and bitten any cheetah that came near. But still, something was wrong. He didn't feel brave. When he walked out into the woods alone, he still felt scared. When he heard a stick break in the forest, he still felt scared. Why even a tiny bird had scared him out of his mind when he was walking back from the attack. He decided there was no one better to ask for help than the bravest of all—the leader of the pride.

When all of the other lions had slipped off to bed and the leader lay alone by the fire, Lewis walked up to him. "I hope you feel better soon, sir. I just had a question to ask you." The leader smiled and nodded. He was the most patient of all the lions and Lewis loved talking to him. "I have never felt brave," Lewis began, "but I know I am a lion and I know that I need to be brave."

The leader nodded and Lewis kept talking. "I have now done three brave things: I hunted the gazelles, I scared off the hyenas, and now I chased away the cheetahs."

The leader of the pride interrupted Lewis. "Yes, those things were very brave. You are indeed a very brave lion. I don't understand why you are having a problem."

Lewis sighed. "Even after doing all of those brave things, I don't feel brave. When I walk alone to my bed at night, I still jump when I hear the crickets."

The leader of the pride laughed, but it was a kind laugh. "Being brave doesn't mean you aren't scared of anything. Why even I jump when I hear the crickets sometimes. Being brave means that when you are scared of something, you face your fear. All creatures are scared, Lewis, even the great lion. The difference between a brave creature and a not-so-brave creature is what you do when you are scared."

Lewis decided that from that day onward, he would be the bravest of all the lions. It didn't matter if he was scared. What mattered was what he did whenever he was scared.

Summer break came to an end and all of the young lions went to school. Lewis liked school and he liked spending time with his friends, but going to school meant that he could not do brave things.

What was there to do at school that would make him brave? To be brave, you had to have danger to face and scary animals to chase away. You had to have cheetahs and hyenas and terrifying creatures that could tear a cut in your side.

Because of this, school was boring to him. Each day, he couldn't wait for the principles loud roar which meant he was able to go be brave. He would race home as fast as he could, set down his bag, and set out in search of danger. If there was a buffalo or a warthog wandering too close to his home, he would roar as loud as he could and chase them away. If he heard one of those strange human vehicles that flew through the sky, he would chase it until it disappeared into the distance. He loved chasing these strange machines; they were so scared of him.

In this way, Lewis the lion tried to prove his bravery to himself and all those around him in every way that he could. He was still scared sometimes, but that didn't matter as long as he acted bravely.

That week, while Lewis was sitting in class daydreaming about all the brave things he would do later, a new student sat down in the seat next to him. "Hello," said the new lion.

Lewis looked up, noticing him for the first time. "Hi." He wasn't in a talking mood, so he didn't say anything else. He was too busy thinking about the cheetah chase and how bravely he had acted.

"What's your name?" asked the new student.

"I'm Lewis," said Lewis, and held out his paw to introduce himself.

"I'm Stevie," said the new lion, but didn't hold out his paw. What Lewis hadn't noticed was that the new student didn't have a paw. Both of his front arms were missing!

Seeing this, Lewis quickly took back his paw. "I'm sorry," he said.

He didn't speak with Stevie for the rest of the class. He was too embarrassed.

Over the next few weeks, Lewis did many brave things outside of school. He climbed a tree to rescue a lion cub. He chased away more cheetahs and hyenas. He even sounded the alarm and helped his pride chase away another group of lions. His parents were very proud of him and his friends respected him more than ever.

School, however, was more boring than ever before. He just couldn't seem to focus. He couldn't stop thinking about all the brave things he was going to do when he went home.

That day, he noticed Stevie sitting alone at lunch. The other lions didn't like to hang out with him because he was missing his front two arms. Lewis liked Stevie, but he knew that if he hung out with Stevie, the other lions would make fun of him just like they made fun of Stevie. Even though he wanted to go talk to Stevie and keep him company, Lewis decided not to.

The next day, Stevie was still alone. And the next. And the next.

Lewis wanted to talk to him more than ever, but he really didn't want to get made fun of, so he didn't.

Then, one day, Lewis noticed the school bullies were gathered around Stevie. They had their arms behind their backs and were trying to eat like Stevie, laughing and making faces at him. Stevie did not look happy. Lewis had always been taught to mind his own business, so he kept eating his lunch. Besides, he had big, brave things to do when he got home from school; he couldn't waste his time worrying about unimportant things.

The bullying of Stevie went on for days and days, and finally, Lewis had had enough. He didn't want to do anything about it, but he did want it to stop. He didn't know what to do so he decided to ask the leader of the pride.

He found him by the fire one night, licking the cut on his side. The cut was much better and the leader was moving around easily once again. "Sir," said Lewis. The leader turned to him and Lewis continued. "I am a brave lion with many important things to do, but I have a problem. At school, there is a lion without any arms. He gets bullied every day and I want it to stop, but I have too many important things to do and I know shouldn't worry about him. What should I do?"

The leader of the pride smiled. "The bravest things we do in life don't happen in the chase or the hunt, Lewis. The bravest things happen in the choices we make every day. It is one thing to roar loud and run fast, another to stand up for what we believe in. If you think this lion is being bullied, the bravest thing you can do is help him. Being brave is about living by what you believe in."

Lewis went home and thought about what the leader of the pride had said. *Is it true?* he thought to himself. *Can I be brave at school just like I can during a chase?*

The next day, when the bullies went over to make fun of Stevie, Lewis stood in their way. "Leave him alone, guys. He's just trying to eat."

Lewis had chased cheetahs and hyenas. He had climbed the tallest trees and hunted the scariest animals. He had chased airplanes and fought off other lions. But standing up to these bullies was the bravest thing he ever did.

THE BOY WHO GAVE WHEN HE HAD NOTHING TO GIVE

Once upon a time, there sat a city high on a large hill. Its walls were thick stone and its towers shimmered in the starlight when the sun went down. Anyone who passed on the road far below looked up at the city in awe. There was nothing quite like it.

"Surely," they would say, "everyone who lives in that city has everything they could ever want."

And it was true—the city was very, very rich. Most who lived there had large houses and many, many servants. They had gardens and fruit trees with more fruit than they could ever eat. They had robes woven with gold thread and rooms filled with the most expensive jewels in the whole world. Like anyone who passed on the road thought, most of the city lived in perfect comfort.

But not all of the city. There was a part of the city that no one saw and no one cared to see. There was part of the city that had no servants, no fruit trees, and no jewels. In fact, they had hardly anything. This part of the city ate rotten fruit when they could find it and wrapped themselves in rags when the bitter cold came over the land. At night, when the rich lords and bankers were warm in their beds, this part of the city came out to find food to feed their starving children and clean water to wet their dry mouths.

Jonah was part of this city. He was one of those with nothing. It wasn't his fault he had nothing, he was just born this way. His parents had died when he was hardly a boy and he had been left alone on the streets. Many boys as young as him could not survive if they were left alone, but Jonah was a clever boy and so he lived each day.

He knew just where to go and what to do to make his life on the street as nice as it could be. When it rained, he caught the water in his handmade buckets and so he was never thirsty. When the rich man with the orchard by the church finished his dinner, Jonah knew his leftovers would be tossed over the fence to the dogs. If he got there before the dogs, he had at least one meal a day. He knew that begging didn't work for him now that he was not so young and cute. He knew that when the king came through town on his horse, it was best that he hide. He knew that the older boys from the orphanage were not nice, so he stayed away. Jonah knew many things, but most of all, he knew that the best thing he could do was stay out of sight.

And so, each day when the sun came up, that is exactly what he did. He stayed away from the streets and the rich people. He sang songs by the river behind the willow trees, fished, or read a book that the old beggar had given him.

Each day was just like the last and Jonah didn't mind this because he was happy and healthy.

But one day, he realized something. *My life is boring,* he thought to himself. *Everything I do is for myself! I do nothing for anyone else. I'm no better than the bankers and rich lords who live in the rich houses with rich clothes.*

He went to the old beggar man who gave him his books. "Sir," he said, "I just realized that I am a very selfish human being. I do everything for myself and don't think for one second about anyone else."

The beggar laughed. "You're a homeless boy without parents, Jonah. What do you expect to do for others? How can you help someone else when you have nothing of your own?"

"But every human should help other humans," Jonah said. "Look at the rich men in the houses. We don't like them because they don't help anyone. But are we any different?"

"Why, of course we're different!" cried the old man. "We don't have houses or jewels or robes of gold thread! If I had one-tenth of what they have, I would give so much away."

Jonah left the old beggar on his corner and went to the river with the willow trees. The old beggar man was right—they didn't have much. But he was also wrong. Compared to the rich men in the rich houses, they didn't have much. But compared to some, their lives were actually quite wonderful. Jonah had food to eat every day, enough water so he was never thirsty, and a thick blanket to keep him warm at night. By the shoe shop and the church, there was a family with nothing at all. The children cried every day and had nothing to eat. The father was gone begging all day, but hardly earned a cent. And the mother had been sick for as long as Jonah could remember.

Surely the family has a much worse life than me, thought Jonah. *I can help them since I have much more.*

And so Jonah set out to find ways that he could help the family.

He started with food. Each day, when the rich man with the orchard by the church finished his dinner, Jonah took the scraps that were thrown over the fence and brought them to the family.

He was a shy boy and he knew that it was better if no one saw his good deed, so he would place the food by the family's cardboard house in the middle of the night so they would discover it in the morning.

If ever he caught a fish down at the river, he would gut it, clean it, and leave it outside of the house of the poor family.

After a week or so, Jonah noticed that the children of the family had stopped crying. He could even hear them laugh sometimes. This made him very happy.

But the mother was still sick and this was not happy. If she didn't get help soon, she would die and leave the father and children all alone. Jonas couldn't let that happen, but he also didn't know how to make her better. He wasn't a doctor and he certainly didn't have the money to pay a doctor.

But he was a clever boy and he knew how to think. *If I can figure out why she is sick,* he thought, *maybe there is something I can do to help her.*

And so, each day after his fishing, he climbed the wall that looked over the courtyard by the church. He sat and watched the family, but especially the mother.

For many days, he sat and watched them until finally, he noticed something. When the weather got worse, the mother would begin to get better. When it rained for many days and there was no sun in the sky, she would begin to recover. But when it was bright and sunny for many days at a time, she would cough and lay on her cardboard mat for hours. Jonah didn't know why at first, but as the days went on, he began to understand.

Each day that it rained, the family would collect water in buckets for them to drink. Most days, it hardly rained at all and the family would have very little water to drink. Those days, the children would drink first, then the father, then the mother. Most of the time, there wasn't enough water for all of them and the mother would drink from the river instead. But if it rained a lot, there was enough rainwater for all of them and they could all enjoy clean water.

She's drinking from the river, thought Jonah. *That's what is making her sick. Of course!*

With that, he set off to get them more water. Each day that it rained, he set up his buckets and gathered water for the family. When the night came, he snuck over to their cardboard hut and set the water beside it.

After another week, the mother of the family seemed to be recovering. She spent very little time in bed and she never went down to the river to get water. She smiled and laughed and danced with her children every day.

The children were happier too. Each day that passed, Jonah noticed them getting healthier and healthier. Their eyes weren't so dark and sad anymore, their mouths weren't so dry, and their stomachs were full of food.

One day, when Jonah went to the wall to watch them, they were gone. Their cardboard hut was still there, but the whole family was gone.

Jonah was a little bit worried, but he knew just who to ask. The old beggar who sat at the gate of the city saw all who came in and all who left. He knew everything that everyone in the city was doing and he would know just where the family was.

"Sir," said Jonah, tugging on the beggar's rags. The beggar turned and looked at Jonah with surprise. He hadn't seen him in a very long time since Jonah had been busy with the family.

"My boy!" he exclaimed. "You've gotten quite skinny! What's wrong?"

Jonah was about to explain how he hadn't eaten in two days and how he had been feeding the poor family, but he decided not to. He knew that it was better to do good deeds in silence and to tell no one.

Instead, he asked the question he had come to ask. "Where is the poor family that lives by the church? They are no longer living in their hut."

The old man smiled. "Ah. The mother, I hear, has healed miraculously, so they no longer have to spend all the father's money on medicine. He bought a shovel and has gotten a job working for a farmer. They have moved into a real house in the village. But what a pity it is that you are so skinny, Jonah!"

"What a pity," said Jonah, and walked down the road with a smile.

SAM THE SLOTH

If you have ever spoken to a sloth, you know just how boring it can be. One sentence can take five whole minutes.

This wouldn't be an issue if sloths were quiet creatures like raccoons and beavers, but they love to talk. Sloths love stories more than anything.

This is how it was with the sloth tribe that lived in the cluster of trees by the river. Each day, they spent six hours listening to one sloth tell a story. There were about one hundred sloths in the tribe, so each sloth told a story once every one hundred days. This was perfectly all right with the sloths because interesting things that would make good stories only happened a few times a year.

Today's story was told by one of the best storytellers of all the sloths. He was telling the most brilliant story of how he once found two apples in one day. "Sooooooooooooooooo thennnnnnnn," he said, and began to reach for a

49

leaf. The rest of the sloths waited as he picked up the leaf, held it to his nose, sniffed it, and put it back down. Then, he picked up another, sniffed it, smiled, and began to move it towards his mouth. He bit it, chewed it, smiled again, and continued to chew it.

A human being could have taken a whole nap or gone for a short walk in the time it took him to come up with his next words. "I foooouuuuuunnnd annnnnnooooother apppppple."

The sloths clapped and smiled. This was a fabulous story. Any of them with really good memories remembered that they had heard this same story one hundred days ago. No one seemed to mind though; this was a very interesting story and they could hear it one hundred times and still not be bored.

When the sloths had had their fill of clapping and the sun was beginning to make its way down, they started their journey back to bed. It was only six in the evening, but bedtime was in three hours, so they would need to hurry back if they were to make it in time. The storytelling tree was almost twenty feet from the sleeping tree.

Sam was a member of this tribe of sloths and he was no different from the rest of them. His favorite things to do were eat, sleep, and listen to stories. Well, he thought these were his favorite things to do, but he couldn't be sure because he had never actually tried doing anything else.

Sam's turn to tell a story was in four days and he was a little bit worried. The last time he had told a story, all the sloths had loved it. He had told the story of how a fly had landed on his nose. Then, he went on to tell how it flew away. It was one of his favorite memories and he still thought about it every day.

This time, however, Sam the sloth didn't know what story he would tell. Nothing very interesting had happened to him in the last ninety-six days, and he was beginning to worry that he wouldn't have a good story to tell when his turn came.

He knew many great stories about all sorts of other creatures, but he was just a sloth. All the heroes of old were men. Sloths didn't do anything important.

He was worrying when he lay down to sleep and when his eyes finally shut, he was still worrying.

What could he tell a story about?

When he woke up, he realized something. *None of the heroes of old woke up and tried to make a cool story,* he thought. *They just lived adventurous lives and the stories made themselves. They tried new things. They did things that no one had ever done before. I need to do something that no sloth has ever done.*

The cluster of trees that the sloths lived in was right next to a large river. Legend had it, that once upon a time, a brave sloth had journeyed all day to the edge of the river. When he got there, it was said that he dipped his finger in the water and tasted it.

This was one of the craziest sloth stories of all and when it was first told, no one believed it was true. In fact, to this day, most sloths thought it was more of a legend than anything.

Sam thought that if he could journey down to the river and do the same thing, he would have a legendary story to tell in three days. *He* would not make the same mistake as the sloth who had gone before, though. He would bring back a pebble from the river as proof of his quest.

And so, determined to have the best story of all, Sam the sloth packed a few leaves in his bag, and set off towards the river early in the morning.

By noon, he had made it all the way to the bottom of the sleeping tree. He was very happy with his progress, so he stopped for three hours and enjoyed a leaf.

By six, he was almost halfway to the river. He could already hear it rumbling over the rocks. He could hear it from the sleeping tree too, but now he heard it a little bit louder.

When the sun had set and it was completely dark, Sam began to wonder if he should have left more time for his journey. He thought about turning back, but he realized that if he turned back now, he would reach the sleeping tree by noon the next day.

He decided that the best thing he could do was sleep on the ground. He had never slept on the ground before, but it would make a good story.

When the sun came up, he got up and continued making his way to the river. He could still see the story tree and the sleeping tree, but they were smaller than before. He had never been so far away from home.

When the sun was high in the sky, Sam the sloth reached the river. It was fast and blue and he had never seen anything like it. He could see it quite easily from his tree, but now he saw it bigger.

He smiled to himself and raised his finger to dip it in the great flowing water.

Suddenly, he heard a cry that scared him out of his mind.

Out of the corner of his eye, he saw an angry mother goose. A great crow was diving out of the sky towards her, trying to steal the egg from her nest.

She hissed and spat and bit, but the crow was not afraid. Finally, she had had enough and she began to chase the crow away from her nest, biting at his tail and honking like nothing you have ever heard.

Sam the sloth was happy because he thought she had won. But then, he saw something that made the smile leave his face.

Another crow was circling above, gazing down at the egg in the empty nest. Sam saw the crow smile and he knew that he had to do something. If he did nothing, the mother would return to an empty nest.

The crow began to dive.

Without thinking, Sam began to sprint towards the nest. It was five feet away and he did not think he could make it in time. He sprinted faster than any sloth had ever sprinted. He ran without looking. He ran so fast that the five feet passed in only thirty seconds.

The crow was almost to the nest when Sam the Sloth dove on top of the egg and covered it with his body.

The crow smashed into Sam with a crunch and his side exploded with pain. He heard the bird screech in anger and he felt claws and beak tear into his body. Afraid that his eyes would be poked out, he covered his face with his arms and clenched his jaw.

He had never felt so much pain in his life, but he knew he didn't have a choice. A quicker animal could have fought the crow, but Sam knew that he didn't have a chance. He was a sloth and sloths are slow.

All he knew is that if he moved, the egg he was protecting would be torn away from its mother. He couldn't let that happen.

All he could do was take the pain until the mother goose returned.

When the mother goose finally came back, she hit the crow so hard that he was knocked senseless. When he awoke, he flew away as fast as he had ever flown. Never had he run into such a brave goose. And never, ever, ever, had he run into such a brave sloth.

Sam was bleeding all over his body and was in more pain than ever before. But he also felt something else that he had never felt before. He felt a sense of pride and worth that he didn't know was possible.

When he returned to his tribe and told the story, the sloths could hardly believe it. His bloody back and shoulders were the only thing that convinced them.

His story was the best story any sloth has ever told to this day.

But to Sam, it is so much more than a story. To Sam, it is a mother goose with a baby goose and a feeling of pride like he has never felt before.

THE GREAT RACE

It was the year 4022 and the world was a crazy place. There were no roads and no cars and people traveled around with jetpacks, zipping about in the sky like bees. Earth's atmosphere had collapsed and there was no more air to breathe, so the population of the whole Earth wore suits that gave them air.

Martin Beasley lived with his mother and father in this strange land. He had no brothers or sisters because having brothers and sisters was not something that people had these days. He spent most of his days inside their house, tending to their plants while his parents were at work.

Plants you see, were very rare these days. Plants were more valuable than gold and the more you had, the more powerful you were in the world. The Beasleys had four plants and it was Martin's job to make sure that every day while his parents were at work, the plants got the light and food they needed to survive.

Martin's family was not poor by any means, but neither were they rich. They had what they needed to survive and they didn't ask for anything more.

But one day, disaster struck. While moving a heavy box at his work, Martin's father, Mr. Beasley, fell and broke his leg.

When he returned home, he was in a terrible state. He limped into the living room and tried to smile at Martin, but his teeth were gritted in pain.

"What's wrong, Father?" Martin cried, setting down the watering can he was holding.

Mr. Beasley slumped into an empty chair and groaned in pain. "I've hurt myself, my boy. It looks bad. The doctor says I'll have to put a cast on it for two months."

"Two months!" Martin said. "Will you be able to work?" Without his father's work, Martin knew that their family would not have enough money to live.

His father tried to smile again. "We'll figure something out."

When Mrs. Beasley got home from her job, she set about making a cast for the injured leg. Martin saw how both his mother and father tried to stay busy to hide the worry in their hearts.

Without his father's work, their family was in trouble.

A week passed, and Mr. Beasley could hardly get out of bed. Each day, he put a smile on his face and hobbled out the door as if to go to work. But after only a few steps, his leg would give out and he would stumble to the ground with a grunt.

The next week, Mrs. Beasley convinced him to stay in bed and stop trying to go to work. "You're only making it worse," she said.

"But we need money, darling," Mr. Beasley replied.

"The money will only come when your leg is better. Now go get back in bed."

Martin's father did as he was told, but Martin saw just how worried both of his parents were.

On market day the next week, Martin's mother walked into the garden room where Martin was watering the four plants. Without saying a word to Martin, she picked up one of the plants and put it in her bag.

Martin was about to ask what she was doing, but he saw the sad look on her face and he knew just what she was doing and how difficult it was to do it. She was about to sell one of the four plants that they had owned for many years.

They didn't have a choice. They needed money and the plants were their most valuable possessions.

The last time they had sold one of their plants, Martin had been only a baby. A fire had ripped through the town and half of their house had burnt to the ground. They sold on plant and were able to repair the house.

Martin knew just how serious it was to sell a plant.

A couple of weeks passed and Martin's father was still not recovering. Mrs. Beasley started waking up earlier each day to earn extra money for the family, oftentimes returning home just before Martin was going to bed. She looked stressed and worn and Martin knew that she could only do this for so long.

After another week and still no signs of recovery from Mr. Beasley, they sold another plant. Even with the money that the plants brought in, the Beasleys had stopped eating meat or anything of any value. For breakfast, they ate oats and fruit. For lunch, rice. And for dinner, leftover rice (if there was any left).

Martin felt hungry every day, but he knew that complaining would do no good for his family.

One day, Mrs. Beasley returned home from her job with a terrible cough. She had only been sleeping for a few hours each night and the difficulty of her life was beginning to make her sick.

Martin knew he had to do something. His father was not getting any better and he would never get better if they didn't get the money to get him to a real doctor. His mother's cast was helping, but it wasn't enough. If Mr. Beasley's leg healed as it was now, it would be crooked and he would never be able to walk again.

His father was hurt and his mother was sick and they had no other family to help them. Martin knew that it was up to him.

The next day, when he woke up in the morning, he set about finding ways to make money for his family.

First, he tried knocking on his neighbor's doors and asking if he could clean their jetpacks. Most turned him away, but two said yes. He was proud of himself when he returned home late at night with two small coins. But when he saw his injured father sleeping in the chair, he realized just how little money it was and just how many jetpacks he would need to clean to help his family.

Each jetpack he cleaned got him one coin. To pay for a doctor to fix his father's leg, he would need ten thousand gold coins. Martin knew that it would take him his whole life to clean ten thousand jetpacks.

And so, after a few days of cleaning jetpacks and a few more coins, he decided to try something new. He walked to the robot yard and tried to talk to one of the guards. "Excuse me, sir," he said, "is there any way I could get a job in this robot yard?"

The guard looked at Martin and laughed. Martin was only twelve years old. No twelve-year-old worked a normal job. "You really think

I'm going to let a little boy work in a robot yard? You'll get killed."

He laughed again and pushed Martin out the door. The robot yard *was* a very dangerous place, even for grown men. The guard was mean, but he was probably right. It was too dangerous for a boy.

But how am I ever going to make money? thought Martin. *My family needs my help, but it seems there's nothing I can do. I'm just a boy.*

Suddenly, something caught his eye. On a billboard high in the sky, Martin could read the words:

THE GREAT RACE WIN 20,000 COINS! RISK LIFE AND LIMB FOR THE BIGGEST PRIZE OF ALL!

Twenty-thousand coins! thought Martin. *Twenty Thousand coins would be enough to get a doctor for my father's leg and buy back the plants we sold.*

Martin didn't know what sort of race this was or when it was, but he did know that he could save his family if he won. He knew that he had to find out more about this race and find out how to win.

The next day, he went to the tallest building in the whole city where all the most important people worked. "I want to enter into the Great Race," he said to the man at the desk.

The man laughed just like the guard had, and Martin knew that he would tell him how foolish he was. But surprisingly, he didn't. "You want to enter the great race? How wonderful. How entertaining that will be. A little boy going up against grown men!"

The man gave Martin a blue tag with a number on it, then a small piece of paper with a bunch of words. Martin didn't understand what the words said, but he knew he needed the money more than anything, so he signed his name on the line. "Wonderful," said the man at the desk. "Now, I'm assuming you've raced jetpacks before, obviously? You know how it all works?"

"Of course," lied Martin, and left the building. He didn't even know that you *could* race with jetpacks. Jetpacks were extremely dangerous if you started going too fast and it would be very stupid to race them.

The race was in a week and Martin knew that he needed to practice if he was going to even know how to race. So, when his father was asleep and his mother was away at work, he took out his father's old set of jetpacks and strapped it onto his back.

He had never tried to go fast on a set of jetpacks, so when he pulled down on the lever and shot into the sky, he couldn't believe it. The wind screamed past his face and his eyes watered from the speed. He felt scared, but he knew he couldn't let his family down.

When he got home later that day, he snuck his father's jetpack back into the closet and tended to the two plants in the garden room. He didn't like hiding things from his parents, but he knew that if they found out what he was training for, they wouldn't let him race. He needed to race. They needed him to race. Without this race, there was no hope.

He practiced every day for the next week, and when the day of the race came around, he felt like he knew what to do.

But when he saw his competitors, he wasn't so sure. They were fully grown men with jetpacks that were much nicer than his. They had helmets and armor that would protect them if they fell. They had spikes on their arms to puncture the other racers' jetpacks and huge shields to push them away.

Martin felt tiny with his jetpack on the starting line. The men around him grunted and yelled curses at each other and the crowd cheered and laughed. They had never seen such a small and timid-looking racer. Martin had no armor, no spikes, and no helmet—just an old jetpack and a lot of courage.

When the horn sounded and the racers took off, Martin was left in the back. At first, he didn't mind. He knew that he couldn't get run over if he was in the back. But then, he remembered the twenty thousand coins and his father's broken leg and he pulled down on the lever and shot forward.

After a few minutes of racing, he noticed something interesting that he didn't expect. He thought being small and young was a bad thing, but it was also a good thing. The other racers didn't seem to notice him at all! They were so busy ramming into one another and yelling curses that it seemed they didn't even see the twelve-year-old boy with the old jetpack trailing behind them.

Martin knew that if he was going to win, it would not be by knocking the other racers out of the way. He would have to win by staying out of the way.

And so, when the first lap came to an end after a few more minutes, Martin made sure to keep quiet and out of the way. The other racers rammed into each other and many were knocked to the ground far below. They screamed and kicked and hit each other with their spikes. But none of them noticed the little boy on the old jetpack who stayed right behind them.

When the second lap finished, there were only six racers left. Martin was one of them. He had one more lap to win twenty thousand coins and save his family.

Halfway through the lap, two of the racers got in a ramming battle and went tumbling to the ground. Now, there were only four left. Martin, and three more.

All the others were in front of him and he could see them looking at each other angrily as they raced along. They started yelling and cursing, and as they rounded the final curve, they all came crashing together. They kicked and screamed and pulled each other back, trying desperately to get to the finish line first.

What they didn't notice in all the uproar and noise, was the little boy with the old jetpack that raced around them and across the line.

When Martin got home that night, his mother was crying. When he walked into the room, she tried to hide her tears, but Martin saw them very clearly. "Oh Martin, we just don't have enough. We won't be able to fix your father's leg. It's all for nothing."

Martin smiled a big smile and set his bag down with a thud. Mr. and Mrs. Beasley looked up and he unzipped the bag and dumped out twenty thousand gold coins.

Their jaws dropped.

HAMSTEAD AND HERMIE

Once upon a time, there were two brothers named Hamstead and Hermie. They lived in a town by the river. Their town was named Door. No one knew why it was named Door, but no one seemed to care. On the other side of the river sat another town. This town's name was Boor. No one knew why it was called Boor, but once again, no one seemed to care.

A bridge crossed the river and ran between the towns of Door and Boor, but no one knew why it was there because no one ever crossed it. When Hamstead and Hermie were very young, they asked their mother and father why no one ever crossed the bridge. They thought it was a good question, but it seemed that neither of their parents agreed because they responded very angrily.

"No one crosses the bridge," their father said, "because no one wants to cross the bridge. No Doorians care to see Boor and no Boorians care to see Door. That's how it is, and that's how it should be."

The bridge didn't have a name. It was just called "the bridge".

Hamstead and Hermie tried to learn about Boor as they grew up, but it was very difficult. Nobody seemed to know anything about this town on the other side of the river. Every time they brought up Boor, or the Boorians, or mentioned crossing the bridge to see what it was like on the other side of the river, the adults would frown and send them to time-out.

"Why does everyone hate Boor so much?" Hamstead asked Hermie one day.

"I don't know," replied Hermie. "Maybe the Boorians did something very bad to the Doorians long ago."

"Or," said Hamstead, "maybe the Doorians did something very bad to the Boorians a long time ago."

Each day when they walked to school, the brothers would look across the bridge and wonder what was on the other side. On a clear day, if the sun was out and the fog was gone, they could sometimes see the shapes of buildings and trees far away. One time, when they were very young, Hermie said he saw a dog running by the edge of the river on the other side. Hamstead told Hermie that he was lying, but really he was just jealous of his brother.

When they were seven years old and were no longer scared of the dark, Hamstead and Hermie agreed that they needed to see what was on the other side of the river. The bridge, they thought, meant that some time long ago people had traveled back and forth between the two towns. They wanted to be the first people to cross the bridge since long ago.

So one moonless night, when the town was sleeping and no one could hear their footsteps or see their shadows, Hamstead and Hermie snuck out of their house. They tip-toed down the cobblestone street and to the great bridge. Holding hands, they stepped onto the wooden beams of the bridge and started across it.

They could feel the breeze coming off the moving water and hear the *splish splash* of river creatures far below. Soon—sooner than they expected—the lights of Boor began to shine bright. When they turned around, they realized that the lights of Door were getting dim. They were closer to boor than they were to Door.

When they reached the other side of the river, it was not like they expected. They expected something strange and mysterious—maybe even magical. They thought it would be dangerous and that when they returned to Door, they would have strange stories to tell.

Instead, they found a town much like their own. There were houses and trees, and dogs barked and ran throughout the town. There was a blacksmith's shop and a baker's shop. There were cafes and bookshops and gardens and parks here and there.

The brothers found an inn that was still serving food and decided to have a look inside. They peeked through the windows at first and were disappointed to find normal human beings inside. They had talked before coming to Boor and agreed that Boorians must look like aliens— with big eyes and long necks and mouths that hung open and drooled.

"Do you want to go inside?" whispered Hermie. He was the more adventurous of the brothers. It has been his idea to cross the bridge in the first place.

Hamstead's eyes grew wide. "Into the inn?"

"Where else?" replied Hermie, rolling his eyes.

Hamstead cracked his knuckles and peeked through the window again. He gritted his teeth. "What if they eat us?" he asked. He acted like he was joking, but he wasn't. These Boorians could be some very strange people.

"If they eat us," Hermie said, "then at least there will be a good story about us."

Hamstead frowned. "But they'll never know what happened to us back in Door."

"They will here, though," said Hermie, beginning to walk towards the door. "That'll be a great story."

Before Hamstead could stop his brother, Hermie reached the door to the inn and pulled it open. Hamstead joined him and the two brothers walked in together.

The inn went quiet and the brothers froze. Everybody stared. They didn't want to know what would happen next. "What are two young boys doing out and about at this late hour?" asked the innkeeper.

Hermie puffed up his chest and smiled, continuing to walk in—trying to get lost among the tables and chairs and the legs of the grown-ups that filled the inn. "We're just looking for some food. Mom ran out of food and sent us here, didn't she?" Hamstead nodded and followed his brother close behind.

The innkeeper kept an eye on the boys as they made their way to the counter. Just before they reached him, a small boy pulled them to the side and pushed them into the darkness under the counter. "Who are you?" the boy asked. "You may be fooling all these grown-ups, but you aren't fooling me. I know every kid in this town and you aren't one of them."

Hamstead looked and Hermie and the brothers shrugged. This boy seemed smart and they knew they couldn't lie to him. "We're from Door," said Hamstead as quietly as he could.

All three of the children sat silent for a moment as they all thought different thoughts. Hamstead and Hermie waited to see if this boy would get them in trouble while the boy waited to see what these strangers would do to him. When nothing happened, they smiled and hugged.

"A real Doorian!" whispered the boy excitedly. "I knew you weren't as bad as they said."

"A real Boorian!" said Hermie and Hamstead together. "We never thought we'd actually meet one of you."

"What's it like in Door?" asked the boy.

"Well▯" and with that, the three boys started a conversation that would change the worlds of Door and Boor forever.

They talked about their families and their lives in their towns. They talked about their schools and their friends and their pets—they all loved dogs. They talked about what they drank and the chores they did when they were home and what they hated most about growing up in their towns.

When the inn closed and the innkeeper kicked them out onto the street, the boys didn't stop talking. They walked the dark streets of the town and the boy from Boor showed them all of his favorite trees and the best places to hide.

When they had seen the whole town, they made their way to the great bridge and started to walk across it.

When they got halfway, the boys stopped and stared down into the dark water, telling the stories that they were told when they were younger about Door and about Boor and about why they were such bad places. They laughed at the stories and laughed at the bridge that had divided them for so long.

The boys were so excited to meet each other and so excited to share their stories that they forgot about something important. They forgot that when the night ends, the day comes. And when the day comes, the sun comes as well. And when the sun comes, the people of Door and Boor could see them.

When the sun rose and the people of both towns yawned and woke up to get about their jobs for the day, they were shocked to see three boys standing in the middle of the bridge.

When they called to the boys, the boys did not come. Instead, the boys called back to them and told them to come to the middle of the bridge to talk.

After some groaning and complaining, people from both Door and Boor came to the middle of the bridge.

To this day, the towns of Door and Boor have been friendly neighbors. No one knows why they hated each other so much before.

WALTER AND MITCH AND THE GREAT OCEAN RACE

Walter was a blue marlin who lived at the bottom of the sea with all sorts of other sea creatures. A blue marlin is a beautiful blue and silver fish with a long, sharp nose and fins like knives.

Walter was the biggest and most beautiful of all the blue marlins at the bottom of the sea. He loved being a blue marlin because blue marlins are the fastest fish in the whole world.

Each year, when the Great Ocean Race was held, Walter knew that he had a good shot at winning. There were other fast marlins that lived at the bottom of the sea, but for four years in a row now, Walter had won the ocean raced and proved that he was the fastest of all.

Everyone knew that he was the fastest of all. All he needed to do to prove once and for all that he was the fastest marlin to ever race, was win the fifth year in a row. There was another marlin, you see, many years ago, that also won four races in a row. If Walter could win for a fifth time in a row, he would prove that he was faster than the marlin many years ago. The marlin from many years ago had lost his fifth race in a row.

The race was just a few weeks away and every fish and beast at the bottom of the sea was already getting ready. The course was being set up, bets were being made, and racers were training harder than ever before.

Walter was the only racer in his group of friends and he was happy about this. He knew that if one of his friends was a racer, they would have a hard time getting along. Walter, you see, was the most competitive fish in the whole sea. He would do anything to win that race and beat everyone who was standing in his way.

Each morning, he woke up when the first rays of sun shone through the water. He brushed his teeth and did his stretches, then started to train in the field of seaweed by his house. He would practice twists and turns and zigs and zags. He would practice changing directions faster than the eye could see. He would train and train and train and train because Walter knew that he *needed* to win this race and prove once and for all that he was the fastest sea-beast there ever had been.

When his friends woke up a few hours later, they would go to the field and watch Walter train. Walter was very popular and had many friends. He had turtle friends, dolphin friends, marlin friends, crab friends, and even a seahorse friend.

The seahorse's name was Mitch.

Mitch hated that he was a seahorse. He didn't mind being small or looking funny or being carried everywhere by the ocean currents. What he hated about being a seahorse was how slow he was.

No matter how hard he tried to swim fast like his friend Walter, Mitch was slow. He knew that he could never be fast and he hated it.

When he was just a small fry (a fry is what you call a baby seahorse), Mitch's parents had asked him what he wanted to be when he grew up. Mitch's eyes opened wide and he said, "I want to be the greatest racer that ever lived."

Mitch's parents laughed and told him that that was impossible. They told him that no seahorse could ever be as fast as the other fish and that he should come up with a new dream. This was the worst day of Mitch's life—he knew his parents were right, but he didn't want to accept it.

When he woke up each morning and watched Walter train, Mitch couldn't help but be jealous of his friend. He wanted Walter to win the race just as badly as anyone, but he couldn't help but be a little bit sad when he watched his friend train.

One day, Walter finished his training and was getting ready to return home when he saw that one of his friends was still watching him. It was Mitch.

"Howdy-ho, Mitch," said Walter, still catching his breath from his training. "Why do you look so sad today?"

Mitch tried to smile, but he couldn't. "Mmm, it's nothing," he said and started to float away.

Walter cared about all of his friends and he knew when they were feeling good and when they were feeling bad. He caught up to Mitch with one swish of his tail. "Mitch," he said, "I see that something is bothering you. Why don't you just tell me?"

"Do you really want me to?" asked Mitch, turning to his marlin friend.

"Of course I want you to tell me. I'm your friend—friends care when friends are sad."

"Well," said Mitch shyly. "I haven't told anyone this in a very long time and I hope you don't laugh at me." Walter shook his head and Mitch continued. "Ever since I was a fry, I've wanted to be a racer like you. I want to feel the water rush past my face and see rocks and seaweed fly past me. I want to hear the crowd cheering and feel my heart beating faster than ever before. I want to race like you, Walter."

Walter tried as hard as he could not to smile, but he couldn't help it. Seahorses just didn't race—that was a fact. He patted his friend's tiny head with his fin and said, "You're a seahorse, Mitch. You can't change that. The best thing you can do for yourself is learn how to be happy with what you have."

Mitch forced a smile. "I know. It's just hard sometimes. When I watch you race, I want to be like you."

The two friends hugged and swam home together, Walter swimming slowly so Mitch didn't fall behind.

The race was in exactly two weeks and Walter gave his full attention to his training. He woke up even earlier each morning and trained even longer. Not one fish in the whole ocean was training as hard as Walter was.

With each lap he completed and each twist he performed, Walter couldn't help looking out of the corner of his eye at his little seahorse friend.

Mitch was always smiling and clapping and cheering Walter on, but Walter knew just how sad he was inside.

It made Walter feel very bad for his friend, but he couldn't do anything to help him. *He's just a seahorse,* thought Walter to himself one day, *he will never be a racer. It's no use, wasting my energy feeling bad about something that will never change.*

When the day of the big race came around, every fish at the bottom of the sea was gathered to watch. Mitch and all of Walter's friends were gathered close to the starting line, yelling encouragements to their friend and getting ready for him to become the fastest sea-beast of all time.

A minute before the race was meant to start and the madness was meant to begin, Walter dashed over to the sideline where his friends sat. He swam over to Mitch and whispered in his ear. "Do you want to feel what it's like to swim like the fastest fish in the sea?" Mitch was confused, but he nodded. Walter smiled. "Wrap your tale around my sword and hold on tight."

Mitch's eyes went wide and he did what his friend told him to. He wrapped his little body as tightly as he could around Walter's sharp snout and held on for dear life. Just before the countdown began, he looked back at Walter. "Are you sure?" he whispered. Walter smiled and nodded.

The countdown sounded and all of the racers shot off into the water. Mitch felt the water rush past his face faster than ever before. He felt his heart beating like a drum and heard the crowd screaming loud in his ears. He had never felt like this before and he loved it.

Walter swam as fast as he could, but with Mitch wrapped around his snout, he just couldn't swim fast enough. He knew this was going to happen and he smiled.

When the race came to an end, Walter and Mitch came in eighth. Everyone in the crowd was very disappointed. They booed Walter and his strange seahorse friend.

Walter and Mitch didn't mind. They smiled and hugged and laughed like never before. Mitch had never had so much fun in his life and Walter had never felt so good in his life. Maybe Walter wasn't the fastest beast in the whole sea, but he was the best friend in the whole sea.

ALEXANDER AND THE COAT OF MANY COLORS

Alexander was just two years old when his father lost his job and left for Europe to find a new one. Alexander didn't remember what it was like when his family had money. He didn't remember what it was like to have food on the table when he got home from school. He didn't know what it felt like to wear new clothes or to have new toys each Christmas.

His mother tried to give him the best life she could, but times were very difficult. His father had been injured while working his job in Europe and he wasn't able to send home as much money as he had before.

They didn't have the money to pay for heat and electricity, so each night, Alexander and his mother would cuddle next to the fireplace and eat their dinner together.

This was the only life Alexander had known, so he was used to it. He didn't complain when he was cold or when he was hungry. He didn't ask for expensive gifts at Christmas or whine when he didn't get anything for his birthday. He knew his mother was trying as hard as she could and he knew it was pointless to make her life any more difficult than it already was.

His mother already worked three jobs and never slept more than a few hours each night.

Alexander had friends at school and books to read and he didn't need anything more.

There was just one thing in Alexander's life that bothered him. His grandma's birthday was soon and he didn't have a gift for her.

Alexander's grandma was one of his favorite people on the whole planet and he hated that he didn't have anything to give her for her birthday. She was turning ninety years old.

If it had been any other birthday, Alexander wouldn't have minded as much, but the 90th birthday is a big birthday and Alexander knew that he had to find some way to give her something.

One day, while he was visiting his grandma after school, he noticed that she was shivering. "Why are you shivering, Grandma?" asked Alexander.

She stopped shivering and acted as if she were perfectly warm. "Oh, it's nothing, dear. I wasn't shivering."

Alexander rolled his eyes and looked at her bare, wrinkled arms. "You don't have a jacket, Grandma. That's why you're shivering."

She laughed and changed the subject. Alexander knew what he was going to get her for her birthday.

The next day, when he was walking back from school, Alexander stopped by a store with a window full of the most beautiful jackets he had ever seen. The people in the store frowned at him and made mean faces at his dirty clothes and his messy hair. He didn't mind—he was used to it.

He walked up to the counter and looked up at the man working behind it. "Excuse me, sir. How much to buy that jacket in the window?" He pointed to his favorite jacket in the shop—a bright red one with golden buttons.

The man laughed and stopped what he was doing—he was sewing a new jacket. "That jacket there is two hundred and fifty dollars." He went back to his work without looking at Alexander.

Alexander left the shop looking very sad. He had never heard of something costing that much money. He would never be able to get his grandma a good gift.

He went to see his grandma the next day and she was still shivering just as badly. It was clear to him that her old jacket had worn out and she didn't have the money to buy a new one.

When he asked her where her old jacket had gone and why she didn't have a new one, she just laughed and tried her best to act as if she wasn't shivering.

"Are you excited about your birthday?" he asked her, trying to get his mind off of that jacket in the shop and how he would never in his whole life have enough money to buy it for her.

She smiled. "Of course I'm excited."

Grandma's birthday was in just one week and Alexander knew that he had to find some way to get her a jacket. His hopes of buying the red jacket with the golden buttons were gone, but he still wanted to get her something.

That day, while walking home from school, he visited the jacket shop again. He closed his eyes as he entered and tried his best to ignore the wonderful red jacket with the golden buttons. The same man was working at the counter. When he saw Alexander, he scowled. "What do you want this time, boy?" He was sewing another jacket, his fingers working busily.

"Just looking around," Alexander replied, trying his best to ignore the mean man.

"You know you'll never be able to afford anything from this store," the man said. "I don't see the point of looking around." The man picked up some scraps of fabric he had cut off the jacket he was sewing and threw them in the trash.

This gave Alexander an idea. He was about to walk out of the shop, but he stopped himself. "Can I take that fabric?"

The man looked at the boy and laughed. "This stuff I'm throwing away? Why would you want that?" Alexander shrugged. "Well," said the man, "I suppose there's no reason I should say no."

He got Alexander a small bag and crammed the scraps of fabric into it, sliding the bag across the counter with a mocking laugh. "Enjoy your fabric, boy!"

Alexander thanked the man and walked out of the shop. He ran home as fast as he could and got to work. He had one week to teach himself to sew and make the best jacket his grandma had ever seen. Maybe he didn't have two hundred and fifty dollars, but Alexander had two hands and a lot of love in his heart.

Over the next few days, Andrew stopped by the jacket shop many times. Each day, the grumpy man behind the counter had new scraps to give to the strange boy.

He worked as hard as he could each day to learn how to sew. When he was ready, he started stitching the scraps of fabric together one by one. He tried as best he could to make some sort of pattern, but with so many colors and random shapes, it was impossible.

He didn't have time to visit his grandma during this time, but he knew that she would understand once he gave her such a wonderful gift.

A couple of days before her birthday, Andrew realized that he had a problem. His coat was almost finished, but he didn't have any buttons.

After school the next day, he brought his coat into the jacket shop and asked the man if he had any extra buttons. The man laughed out loud at Alexander and told him to leave the store. He told him what a foolish boy he was and asked him not to come back to the store ever again.

Alexander frowned and pulled the coat out of his bag. He set it on the counter and the man's jaw dropped. "You made this?" he asked. Andrew nodded. The man picked up the coat and looked at it closely, recognizing all the scraps of fabric from his own jackets. "I'll tell you what," said the man. "How about you and I make a deal? If you come here each day after school and work for me for a couple of hours, I'll give you all the buttons you want *and* some money to go with it."

Alexander smiled and shook the man's hand. Maybe this man wasn't so grumpy after all.

When Alexander gave the coat to his grandma, she cried. She had never seen something so beautiful.

When he told his mom about his new job and how much money he would make, she cried. With Alexander's new job, his father would be able to move back in with them.

DISCLAIMER

This book contains opinions and ideas of the author and is meant to teach the reader informative and helpful knowledge while due care should be taken by the user in the application of the information provided. The instructions and strategies are possibly not right for every reader and there is no guarantee that they work for everyone. Using this book and implementing the information/recipes therein contained is explicitly your own responsibility and risk. This work with all its contents, does not guarantee correctness, completion, quality or correctness of the provided information. Misinformation or misprints cannot be completely eliminated.

Made in the USA
Middletown, DE
22 November 2022

15783083R00066